D0559572

Tally Tuttle Turns into a Turtle

CLASS CRITTERS

Book 1

Tally Tuttle Turns into a Turtle

By Kathryn Holmes
Illustrated by Ariel Landy

AMULET BOOKS • NEW YORK

Library of Congress Cataloging-in-Publication Data
Names: Holmes, Kathryn, 1982- author. | Landy, Ariel, illustrator.
Title: Tally Tuttle turns into a turtle / Kathryn Holmes ; [illustrations by Ariel Landy].
Description: New York : Amulet Books, 2021. | Series: Class critters ; book 1 | Audience: Ages 6 to 9. | Summary: Tally Tuttle, a shy, new-in-town second-grader, magically transforms into a turtle on the first day of school, and in order to transform back to herself she must learn how to come out of her shell both literally and figuratively. Includes ten fun facts about painted turtles.
Identifiers: LCCN 2020051896 | ISBN 9781419755675 (hardcover)
Subjects: CYAC: Bashfulness—Fiction. | Turtles—Fiction. | First day of school—Fiction.
Classification: LCC PZ7.H7358 Tal 2021 | DDC [Fic]—dc23
LC record available at https://lccn.loc.gov/2020051896

Book design by Marcie Lawrence

Printed and bound in U.S.A.
10 9 8 7 6 5 4 3 2 1

ABRAMS The Art of Books
195 Broadway, New York, NY 10007
abramsbooks.com

For Evie

Butterflies for Breakfast

It was the first day of school, and Tally Tuttle's stomach hurt.

She sank into the soft leather of the back seat as her big sister, Scarlett, jumped out of the car, shouting, "Bye, Mom! Come on, Tally!"

Scarlett didn't seem nervous at all. Maybe Tally was nervous enough for both of them. She felt like she'd eaten two helpings of butterflies for breakfast. They were tickling her insides with their fluttering wings.

Tally stared at the entrance to the school. The building was taller than her old elementary school—three stories instead of only one. It cast a long shadow across the drop-off area. But the size of the building wasn't the scariest part. The scariest part was not recognizing a single face in the crowd, other than her sister's.

Maybe Tally could imagine her way out of being scared. That was her dad's suggestion. Whenever she felt wobbly or overwhelmed, he told her to try imagining something that would make her smile.

She imagined letting all of the butterflies inside her fly free. She imagined them flocking around the kids and grown-ups outside

the school. She imagined everyone's mouths falling open as the colorful creatures landed on their heads and shoulders and in the palms of their hands.

She felt a giggle bubble up, delicate as a butterfly's wings.

Her mom was watching her from the driver's seat. "Ready to go, pumpkin?"

Tally nodded, but she still didn't move.

"I know you're anxious about not knowing anyone," her mom said gently, "but I also know you're going to make new friends so quickly. A few of my new coworkers have kids in your grade."

Tally's family had moved here one week ago. Tally hadn't finished unpacking. She hadn't found her lucky disco ball keychain or her favorite green nail polish. She was entering second grade with her house key on a plain metal ring, clear sparkle polish on her fingernails . . . and no friends.

The butterflies whooshed back in.

Tally studied her sneakers. They were new, but the same brand and style she'd worn last year. Scarlett had used the move as an excuse to try a whole new look. She was launching into fifth grade in skinny jeans and hot pink, sequined high-tops—a fancy brand that, thanks to their mom's new job, they could finally afford. Tally was wearing new jean shorts and a new green T-shirt, but that was how she'd always dressed. Her straight brown hair was in a ponytail, like always. Her brown eyes were framed by round glasses, like always.

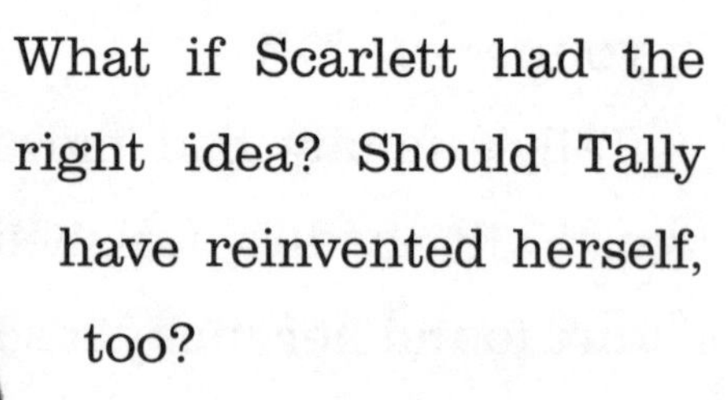

What if Scarlett had the right idea? Should Tally have reinvented herself, too?

What would her new classmates be like? Would she fit in?

What if she didn't?

What if this new place turned out to be perfect for everyone in her family . . . except her?

"Come here." Her mom leaned between the front seats and stretched out her arms. Tally fell into the embrace. Her mom was a fantastic hugger. "I've heard through the grapevine that your teacher this year is amazing," her mom said. "Mrs. Norrell's classroom is supposed to be a really magical place."

That got Tally's attention. "Magical how?"

Her mom's eyes twinkled. "Don't you want to get in there and find out?"

"I guess so."

"Do your best, pumpkin. I'm proud of you no matter what."

"Thanks, Mom." Tally got out of the car and walked to the entrance, where Scarlett was waiting for her. From the curb, their mom honked the horn three times. That was something their dad had come up with,

when he and their mom were dating. “Honk honk honk” before driving away meant “I love you.”

“Honk, honk, honk!” Tally and Scarlett called back together.

Then Scarlett turned toward the door. “Okay, let’s go!”

Tally made herself imagine the silly things that could be waiting for her on the other side of that door. Maybe this school would have murals made of jelly beans decorating the walls. Or maybe her teacher would be an ostrich wearing a tutu.

That one worked. Grinning, Tally followed her sister inside.

Anything but Ordinary

Tally's mom had said Mrs. Norrell's class was supposed to be a magical place, but nothing in here looked particularly magical. The room had desks, chairs, a bulletin board, and posters. There was a guinea pig in a cage by the windows, which was cool, but Tally had had class pets before. In kindergarten, they'd had a fish named Lloyd. In first grade, it was a gerbil named Arabella.

Maybe elementary schools were pretty much the same everywhere.

Aa Bb Cc Dd Ee Ff Gg Hh
Agenda
9:00
10:00
11:00
12:00
1:00
kind
Hard
fun!
READ

But what if there was more to Mrs. Norrell's room than met the eye? Tally imagined the chalkboard swinging away from the wall to reveal a secret passageway. She imagined the hands on the wall clock spinning in reverse, transporting them all back in time. She imagined that the guinea pig was actually a fairy in disguise–

"Take a seat, please, everyone!" Mrs. Norrell called out, making Tally jump.

There was an empty desk with Tally's name on it in the last row. To Tally's left was a Black boy whose desk label read "Nate." The white girl on Tally's right had already peeled off her nametag, but her gold necklace read "Victoria" in swirly letters.

Nate peeked at Tally over the top of his thick book. "You're new." Tally nodded, and Nate said, "Okay." Then he went back to reading, and Tally's hopes for a conversation–or even her first new friend–fizzled out like a firework that never made it off the ground.

Tally turned to her other side. Victoria was complaining about something to the girl in front of her, her voice an angry hiss. When she caught Tally looking at her, she snapped, "What do you want, new kid?"

"Nothing," Tally said, facing straight ahead with flaming cheeks. "Sorry."

"Welcome to second grade. I'm so glad you're all in my class," Mrs. Norrell said from the front of the room. Tally puffed out a relieved breath. At least *someone* was happy to see her. "This is going to be an incredible year," her teacher continued. "I can feel it." She rustled some papers on her desk. "I'll start by taking roll. Aaron Ackerman?"

"Here."

"Becca Barrett?"

"Here."

Tally tried to pay close attention, but it didn't take long for the names to start blurring together. Plus, from her seat in the last row, she couldn't see her classmates' faces. She had a great view of the backs of everyone's heads. The tan, brown-haired boy goofing off in the second row was . . . Gavin? The Asian girl wearing the pineapple-print sundress was . . . Lydia? And the Black girl with the cool braids, next to maybe-Lydia, was . . . Madison?

It felt like a test Tally was destined to fail.

She was concentrating so hard that she missed her own name.

"Tallulah Tuttle? Tallulah, are you with us?"

A wave of giggles swept through the room.

"Here!" Tally squeaked. "Sorry!"

"Tallulah?" someone said.

Tally flinched. It wasn't that she didn't like her full name. It was that "Tallulah" was anything but ordinary. For today, at least, ordinary was what Tally wanted to be. "I go by Tally," she whispered . . . but it was too late.

"Ta-*loooo*-lah!" a boy squawked.

"Ta-*loooo*-lah!" another boy hooted back.

Within seconds, shouts of "Ta-*loooo*-lah! Ta-*loooo*-lah!" danced through the air. Kids were laughing and staring. Mrs. Norrell was darting around the room, looking for the culprits.

Tally sank down in her chair. This was what she had been afraid of. Her mom had told her she'd make new friends quickly.

Her mom had been wrong.

3

Imagining Happier Things

"Ta-*loooo*-lah! Ta-*loooo*-lah! Ta-*loooo*-lah!"

"Enough!" With three loud claps, Mrs. Norrell called the class to order. She frowned at her students. "We do not make fun of our classmates' names—or anything about our classmates, for that matter." Her eyes found Tally's and softened a little. "Tallulah, I apologize. Everyone, say you're sorry to Tallulah."

Tally wished Mrs. Norrell would stop saying her name. The sing-song apology that followed—*We're sorry, Tallulah*—didn't help.

Mrs. Norrell continued taking roll, and then began talking about everything they'd be doing in the second grade. The whole time, Tally felt like her classmates were sneaking glances at her. She thought she could still hear muffled laughter.

She was never going to make new friends now.

Tally felt a rush of missing. She missed her old school. She missed the friends she'd had for years—the people who knew that she preferred to be called Tally, and that she only wanted strawberry jam (never, ever grape jelly) on her PB&Js, and that her favorite kind of green was the happy, minty shade of mint chocolate chip ice cream.

She didn't want to figure out how to fit into a new place. She didn't want to always be imagining happier things. She just wanted to *feel happy*.

Tally felt the prickle of oncoming tears. She squeezed her eyes closed. She couldn't cry on the first day of school. She didn't want to spend the entire year as Ta-*loooo*-lah Tuttle, Cry-Baby. She clenched her fists. She hunched her shoulders and tucked her chin into her neck. She tried her hardest to conjure up something magical and wonderful—something that would make her smile—but her mind had gone blank.

Desperate, she looked around the room for inspiration. Her eyes landed on the class pet. The sign on the cage said the guinea pig's name was Bagel. All Bagel had to worry about was eating and sleeping and digging around

in his bed of wood shavings. He looked content, like he was exactly where he was supposed to be.

Unless he actually *was* a fairy in disguise, like she'd imagined earlier.

Tally wished she could disguise herself as something else. But she knew that magic wasn't real. She sighed.

A gust of wind blew that sigh right back into her face.

There was a popping sound, like the opening of a tightly screwed-on jar lid, followed by a tinkly noise, like someone was playing the two highest piano keys over and over and over.

The air suddenly smelled like citrus fruit and rotten eggs.

Tally blinked. In an instant, the world had changed around her. Her classroom was enormous. So was everyone in it.

No—her classroom hadn't grown bigger. She'd gotten smaller. Much, much smaller. And she was lying on the floor.

Wait. She wasn't lying down. She was standing, but on four legs instead of two. And those legs were short and scaly. And they ended in sharp claws. When Tally told her fingers to wiggle, the claws tapped against the floor.

She slowly, so slowly, craned her neck down until she could see her reflection in the shiny tile. It wasn't a perfect mirror, but it was clear enough to show her the truth.

Tally Tuttle had turned into a turtle.

The Weight of Her Shell

At first, she was sure she'd imagined it. But when Tally shut her eyes, waited several seconds, and checked her reflection again, the same face stared back at her.

She had bulging black eyes. Her normally pale skin was striped in green, yellow, and brown. She could feel the weight of her shell on her back.

She was definitely a turtle, which meant . . . magic was real!

Tally did a happy wriggling dance. Then

she twisted her long neck to look up, up, up at her classmates. The few faces she could see wore matching confused frowns. It was like a photographer had surprised the class by taking a flash photo before they could say "cheese," and they were all still seeing spots.

The room was silent except for the wall clock's tick-tock-ticking.

Then Victoria spoke. "Um." She was looking at Tally's empty chair, far above where turtle-Tally crouched in the shadow of her own mint-green backpack. "Why does it smell weird in here?"

"Where's Tallulah?" Mrs. Norrell approached, her footsteps heavy and echoing on the tile floor. Every step shook Tally from her claws to her broad, flat beak. "Did anyone see Tallulah leave the room?"

"I'm down here!" Tally shouted. Her voice came out as a shrill turtle chirp. The high-

pitched sound was so shocking that Tally instinctively tucked her head and legs into her shell.

Oh. Inside her shell, it was dark and warm. In here, she felt comfortable, cozy, and safe.

She listened with interest as her classmates debated what had happened to her. Thanks to the shell, their voices were muffled. It was like Tally was eavesdropping from deep within a pillow fort.

"I think she was upset," one girl said.

That was true. Tally had been upset. She didn't feel upset anymore.

"You all weren't being very nice," another girl said. "She's new, and she can't help that she has an unusual name. Mrs. Norrell, I told them to stop!"

Someone had stood up for Tally? She hadn't heard that part.

"Maybe she felt sick," a boy guessed.

Did having a belly full of frantic, fluttering butterflies count as feeling sick?

"Sick . . ." Mrs. Norrell said thoughtfully. "Hm. Perhaps . . . perhaps Tallulah went to the nurse. Yes. I believe I heard her ask to be excused." She sounded relieved to have figured it out. "Tallulah went to see the nurse."

Tally did another little dance inside her shell, celebrating her good luck. First, she'd been saved from humiliation. Then, her teacher had come up with the perfect excuse for her absence. Tally didn't know how or why she'd become a turtle. She didn't know why no one in her class seemed to have seen it happen. She didn't understand what was going on *at all*.

But magic was real.

And she wasn't being laughed at anymore.

Those were both very good things.

5

A Strange New World

Tally poked her head out of her shell. Mrs. Norrell was standing beside Tally's chair. The teacher's legs were like the giant sequoia trees Tally's family had seen when they visited California last year. Tally didn't want to get accidentally stepped on, so she decided that her first task as a turtle was to seek cover.

She began to crawl. It was slow going. She wasn't used to walking on all fours, and she had to figure out how to make her right and left sides work in opposition. She passed under Nate's stretched-out legs. She crossed the two floor tiles that lay between Nate's desk and the bookshelf by the wall. She ducked under the ledge of the shelf.

She discovered a strange new world.

Under the bookshelf, there were broken pencils that were longer than she was. Metal paperclips that had been bent into various shapes. Dust bunnies that tickled her nostrils and made her want to sneeze. Even a few treasures: a red Starburst, a glittery beaded bracelet, and a rubber ball that was bright blue with silver sparkles.

Tally used her nose to nudge the Starburst toward the front of the shelf, where she'd be able to find it later. Starbursts were her favorite candy of all time, and red was her favorite flavor. She wouldn't usually eat candy off of the floor, but the Starburst was still tightly sealed in its wrapper. It couldn't hurt to save it, just in case.

Next, she spent several minutes shimmying her body underneath the beaded bracelet until it perched atop her shell like a crown. If she was going to be a turtle, she thought she might as well be a fancy one.

Finally, she returned to the sparkly blue ball. She kicked it gently toward the wall, and it bounced back to her. She turned and aimed at a crumpled-up piece of notebook paper a few feet away. She started to kick, but then got a better idea. She pulled her head back into her shell, and then popped out, ramming the ball with her hard beak.

She missed the wad of paper. The ball hit

something else, instead. Tally slowly made her way toward the whatever-it-was and was delighted when it turned out to be a dusty fidget spinner. She decided to award herself one point for each time the ball hit the toy, and five points if she actually got the spinner to spin. She imagined she was on a game show, competing to win all the Starbursts she could eat.

She was up to seventeen points (seven hits and two spins) when someone spoke: "What are you doing?"

Tally jumped. "Who, me?"

"Yes, you. The turtle. What are you doing?"

"It's a game I made up," Tally said.

"How does it work?"

Tally explained the rules and then asked, "Where are you?" She turned in a circle. "*Who* are you?"

She looked up to see a spider's web running between two legs of the bookshelf. The web was long and skinny, delicately suspended about two inches above the floor. In the corner of the web, tucked into a nook where a wooden leg screwed into the bottom shelf, sat a small, black spider.

"Hello," the spider said. "I'm Clementine."

"Hi." Tally crawled closer. "I'm Tally."

The spider shrank back into her corner. "Are you going to squash me?"

Tally froze. "No. Why would I do that?"

"Lots of people try." Clementine shuddered and her web vibrated in response.

"Well, I won't." Tally had never been a big fan of spiders, but now that she was actually talking to one, she could see that there was no reason to be afraid.

"Glad to hear it." Clementine cocked her head at Tally. "So, tell me: how did you turn into a turtle?"

6

Some Kind of Magic

Tally gasped. "You saw me change?"

"Clear as day. You were sitting in your chair, as a human." Clementine pointed one of her eight feet in the general direction of Tally's desk. "Then, poof! You were on the floor, and you were a turtle! It was extraordinary. How did you do it? Is turning into an animal something people do often?"

Tally had been so busy exploring and playing that she'd almost forgotten she wasn't supposed to be hiding under the bookshelf.

She was supposed to be Tally the person, not Tally the turtle. Remembering the truth sent a whisper of worry slithering under her shell.

"I have no idea how I turned into a turtle," she murmured. "I think it was some kind of magic. How come you saw it happen, but my teacher and classmates didn't?"

"They didn't see you?" The spider's eyes widened with surprise. "I don't know why not. It was quite a spectacle."

"They think I'm visiting the nurse."

"Ah." Clementine moved from one end of her web to the other, looking at Tally from all sides. "Are you planning to change back?"

Tally gulped. She'd been so excited about her transformation–and so relieved not to be the center of her classmates' attention anymore–that she hadn't thought that far ahead. "I don't know how. I–"

"Madison, can you fill Tallulah in when she

returns?" Mrs. Norrell sounded close by. Tally crawled nearer to listen.

"Absolutely!"

Tally recognized the confident voice. This was the girl who'd said she'd told the kids who were making fun of Tally's name to stop. Madison, she recalled, was the Black girl with the cool braids, who sat two desks in front of Nate. Tally was pleased with herself for remembering.

"My dad works with her mom," Madison said, "so I'm supposed to introduce myself anyway. Ooh, can I be in charge of showing her around?"

"Thank you, and yes, of course you can be Tallulah's guide," Mrs. Norrell said. "We want to make our new friend feel welcome. Lydia, do you want to help?"

"Definitely!" Lydia–the girl in the pine-apple dress who sat beside Madison–had a cheerful voice. She sounded like she was

the kind of person who wasn't bothered by anything. Tally was jealous of people like that, the ones her dad said let troubles roll off them "like water off a duck's back." Maybe that's why Tally had turned into a turtle, instead of a duck. When troubles came, she couldn't help splashing around in them.

But maybe hanging out with Madison and Lydia would be like carrying an umbrella and wearing galoshes. Maybe she'd get less wet.

"I'm down here!" Tally called out. "Let's be friends!"

"They won't understand you," Clementine said. "Humans don't speak Animal. To them, you'll sound like a turtle."

"I thought I wasn't going to have any friends because everyone was laughing at me earlier," Tally fretted, "but what if *this* is my chance to make friends? What if I miss it because I'm a turtle?"

"Is that how human friendships work?" Clementine asked. "You only get one chance?"

"I don't know!" Tally let out a frustrated growl and pulled into her shell, where she felt comfortable, cozy, and safe.

"The way I see it," Clementine told her, "you have two options: you can accept that you're a turtle and learn to live like one, or you can figure out how to turn back into a person."

From inside her shell, Tally said, "I don't want to stay a turtle forever."

"Well, I know someone who's been in this classroom a lot longer than I have," the

spider said. “He might have some answers for you.”

Tally poked the tip of her nose out into the dusty air. “Really?”

“Really. But to get to him, you’re going to have to come out of that shell.”

Crawling into the Light

Clementine scuttled along the bottom of the bookshelf. "We have to cross to the other side of the classroom."

Tally hesitated. "Can't we stay here a little longer?" She felt comfortable, cozy, and safe under the bookshelf. "We could play for a while, and then go talk to whoever it is?"

"What if every minute you spend as a turtle means it will be harder to change back?"

Tally let out a squeak of alarm. She hadn't thought of that.

“I can go first, if you’re scared,” Clementine offered.

Tally *was* scared. But she looked into Clementine’s black eyes and saw that the spider was scared, too. Clementine knew people liked to squash spiders. She was afraid it was going to happen to her. As small as Tally was now, as a turtle, she was a lot bigger than Clementine. She was also much less creepy-crawly. Tally thought she had a better chance of making it across the floor in one piece than Clementine did. And yet, Clementine was being brave for Tally.

Tally decided that she could be brave, too.

“No!” she cried, moving as quickly as her squatty turtle legs would let her. “I’ll go first. I’ll make sure the coast is clear.”

Clementine sighed with relief. “Thank you, Tally.”

“You’re welcome.” Tally took a deep breath before crawling into the light. When her eyes adjusted to the brightness, she saw that her

classmates were leaving for the cafeteria. Lunchtime, already! As if on cue, her stomach growled. Tally looked longingly over her shoulder at the red Starburst she'd set aside. It would probably take her an hour to unwrap it with her beak and her clumsy turtle toes. No, lunch would have to wait until after she met Clementine's friend.

The classroom door closed behind Mrs. Norrell.

"It's safe!" Tally said to Clementine. The two of them began their trek across the tile floor. Tally was bigger, but Clementine was faster, so they traveled at almost the same speed.

They'd made it to the center of the room when the door swung open again. Two of Tally's classmates ran in. "Grab your lunch-box before Mrs. Norrell notices we're gone!" shouted one of the boys. He was skinny with light skin and dark hair.

The other boy, blond with glasses, went to a desk in the back row by the windows. While he was rummaging in his backpack, the first boy opened his own lunchbox and pulled out a bag of chips. "Boom!" the dark-haired boy shouted, clapping his hands together to pop the bag, creating an explosion of chip fragments.

"Ahh!" His friend staggered, pretending to be hit by the blast. Then he recovered and tackled his opponent. The two of them slammed into a desk, skidding it across the floor toward Tally and Clementine.

"Quick!" Tally whispered to the spider. "Get inside my shell!"

Clementine was too terrified to respond. The boys' play-fight drew nearer.

"Hurry!" Tally shouted, pulling her right front leg into her shell to give Clementine somewhere to go. This time, the spider jolted into motion. She climbed into the darkness by Tally's shoulder. Her legs tickled Tally's scaly skin, but Tally didn't dare giggle. She pulled the rest of herself inside her shell and held her breath.

She could still hear the boys crashing around. If one gigantic sneaker landed in the wrong spot, or if a desk or chair flipped over, that would be it. Tally and Clementine would be toast.

8

Spinning, Spinning, Spinning

Tally had never lived through an earthquake, but she could imagine it feeling something like this. The floor shook, rocking her from side to side. The desks and chairs roared like thunder as they scooted along the tile. The boys' shouts echoed loudly in the empty room.

"Gotcha!"

"No fair! I wasn't–"

"Take that–"

"Yowch!"

They didn't say anything about a turtle. Tally didn't think they'd seen her yet. But it was only a matter of time.

Clementine was quivering inside Tally's shell, clutching her shoulder with all eight legs. Meanwhile, Tally's tiny turtle heart hammered in her chest. Her breath came in short gasps and her head throbbed. She didn't just have butterflies in her stomach. She was filled, tongue to tail, with angry, buzzing bees—

Thwack!

One of the boys accidentally kicked her. She flew across the floor, out of control. She shut her eyes tight. She was spinning, spinning, spinning, and she didn't know how to stop.

Bam!

Tally ricocheted off something and went

spiraling in a new direction. She felt the glittery bracelet slip from her shell. She heard its beads scatter.

Ping!

She tapped something metallic. A chair leg, maybe.

She was slowing down, but still spinning. She could barely tell her head from her tail. She wasn't sure if she'd ever be able to walk in a straight line again.

"David! Owen! What's going on?"

Mrs. Norrell was here! The teacher sounded angry.

The commotion stopped immediately. "Owen forgot his lunchbox," David said.

"We were just playing around," Owen added.

"Put those chairs back," Mrs. Norrell commanded. "Clean this mess up. We'll be visiting Mr. Angelo's office, and we'll be calling your parents—"

Thud.

Tally hit a wall. The world spun one last time, but the spin felt more up and over than around and around. Then, finally, she was still.

She felt Clementine leave her shell. When she was sure the spider was out of accidental squashing range, she poked out one leg, then another, and then a third and a fourth. Tally wiggled her feet, stretching her clawed toes toward the floor.

Except . . . there was no floor. There was only air.

"Clementine?" Tally stuck her head out of her shell to find that she was floating. The spider was clinging to the ceiling, right by her head. "How am I doing this?" she asked, still dizzy from her Tilt-a-Whirl trip across the floor. "Why are you upside-down?"

"I hate to tell you this, Tally," Clementine whispered, "but I'm not the one who's upside-down—"

"Oh! Where did you come from?"

Tally shrieked in surprise as Mrs. Norrell crouched beside her. She waved her legs frantically, trying to flip over. All she did was shimmy from side to side on her shell.

"Don't be scared," Mrs. Norrell said, giving Tally a warm smile. She looked at the two boys. "Owen, grab me a shoebox from the arts and crafts corner. A tissue as well, please."

"Yes, ma'am." Owen walked away and returned a moment later with an empty box and a Kleenex. "How'd that turtle get in here, anyway?"

"I don't know, but . . ." Mrs. Norrell tapped her chin. "Animals do seem to have a way of following me." She reached toward Tally. "It's okay, little one. I've got you. Let's get you back outside, where you belong."

The Forest of Grass

Using the tissue to shield her fingers, Mrs. Norrell scooped Tally up and flipped her over. She carefully set her down inside the shoebox. Tally squealed and chirped and hissed. "It's me, Tally Tuttle!" she cried. "Don't take me outside, please! There's someone in here I need to talk to!"

Her protests didn't help. The lid began to close over her head. The last thing Tally saw before the darkness was complete was Clementine scurrying up the classroom wall.

"You'll find your way back!" the spider called. "I believe in you!"

Tally felt herself rising into the air. It was like being on a fast-moving elevator. Then the box began to bounce with Mrs. Norrell's foot-steps. A door squeaked open and slammed shut. Mrs. Norrell walked and walked. She shoved her weight into another door, and inside the box, Tally slid into a corner, claws scratching helplessly at the cardboard.

Finally, the box descended, which made Tally feel like the floor was dropping out from under her. Tally wanted nothing more than to pull her legs and head into her shell, but she made herself stand firm. She would be brave and face whatever was about to happen head-on. Clementine believed in her.

The box lid lifted. Sunlight and fresh air streamed in. Mrs. Norrell tilted the box and deposited Tally in a patch of tall grass. "There," she said. "Isn't that better?"

"No!" Tally shouted. "It's not better!"

"Is the turtle safe out here?" David asked, peering down. "Are there predators?"

"Yeah, what if it gets eaten?" Owen chimed in.

"Eaten?!" Tally yelped.

"A turtle's hard shell protects it from most predators," Mrs. Norrell said.

Tally breathed a sigh of relief.

"Where did it come from?" Owen asked. "Was it a pet?"

"This little one probably belongs to the family of painted turtles that lives by the creek. The markings look the same. I bet someone found it and brought it inside to show their friends." Mrs. Norrell frowned. "I do hope they washed their hands. Turtles can carry salmonella germs."

"Salmo-what?" David asked, freezing with his fingers extended to touch Tally's shell.

"Salmonella. It's a type of bacteria that can make you sick to your stomach." Mrs. Norrell got to her feet. "Come along, boys. We still have to visit Mr. Angelo's office to discuss your behavior." She began to walk away, and the boys followed.

Tally was a little insulted that her teacher

thought she was germy. Still, she crawled after Mrs. Norrell, David, and Owen as fast as she could, shouting, "Wait!" It was no use. Even if her tiny turtle legs could keep up, the humans wouldn't be able to understand what she was saying.

Tally was on her own.

She had to get back inside the school. She had to talk to Clementine's friend on the other side of her second-grade classroom. Before she could do that, she had to figure out exactly where Mrs. Norrell had released her. Tally craned her neck to look around. All she could see was green grass and brown dirt. She needed higher ground, so she could get her bearings and come up with a plan.

She began to crawl through the forest of grass. The blades bent as she passed over them and snapped back up as soon as her weight had lifted. She couldn't see farther than a few inches in front of her nose, but she trudged on.

After a couple minutes, she bumped into something hard. Tally staggered back, beak stinging and eyes watering. When she looked at what she'd run into, she forgot about the pain.

The rock was tall, but not too tall for a tiny turtle to climb. It was also craggy, which meant her claws would have somewhere to dig in. Tally took a tentative step onto the warm gray surface, then another, and another. She didn't stop until she reached the summit.

A Sense of Belonging

Tally felt like she had scaled a mountain. She could see for miles and miles.

Well, maybe not actual miles. Turtle-sized miles. She could see the school building and parking lot in one direction, and the playground, with the creek and woods beyond, in the other. Mrs. Norrell had released her on the lawn by the side entrance, a lot closer to the creek than to the school. That made sense, as she thought Tally was a real turtle with a turtle family.

Between Tally and the side door, there was

a stretch of overgrown green grass, followed by a long concrete sidewalk, followed by a set of stairs. There was no way Tally could climb those stairs in her turtle state. Not that it mattered whether she could handle the stairs by herself. She couldn't turn the doorknob, either.

Tally looked over to the playground, where the kindergarteners were having recess. Mrs. Norrell had guessed that someone had brought Tally inside the school building. The teacher was wrong, of course—but maybe the kindergarteners could be useful now. Tally could crawl to the blacktop and try to look irresistible. One of the kids might pocket her and take her to their classroom for show and tell. Kindergarten, first, and second grades were all on the ground floor. Tally could slip away to her own classroom and find Clementine.

It was as good a plan as any.

Okay, so how . . .

Tally yawned.

How should she . . .

She shifted positions, seeking a more comfortable place to plant her feet. The movement felt like crawling through maple syrup. Her tiny body felt heavy and sluggish. Her tiny brain felt foggy and sleepy.

She realized she was kind of cold. But the sun was warm on her shell. The surface of the rock was warm beneath her. It was like being wrapped in a heated blanket.

Tally stretched out her neck as far as it would go, pointing her beak at the sky, and closed her eyes. She knew there was something she was supposed to be thinking about. She could probably think about it later.

For now, all she wanted to do was bask in the beautiful sunshine on this beautiful rock, with the beautiful breeze brushing lightly across her beautiful green-and-brown skin. For the first time since her family's big move a week ago, Tally felt a sense of belonging. Everything in her world felt . . . right.

Time passed.

Tally basked.

Until she heard someone shouting. The voice seemed far away, but it was getting closer. There was a screeching sound, too, and the flapping of wings.

"Look out! Look out!"

Tally slowly peeled her eyes open.

"Hey! Turtle on the rock!"

Tally's brain kicked back on as she realized two important things: one, she was the only turtle on this rock, and two, this was the only rock in this section of the lawn.

"Move, turtle!" whoever-it-was yelled. The voice was coming from the grass to Tally's left. "It's right above you!"

Tally looked up to see a giant crow dropping from the sky. Its black wings were

stretched wide and its sharp talons were extended toward Tally, ready to snatch her up. It opened its beak and let out another ear-piercing screech.

Tally didn't have time to run. As a turtle, she simply wasn't fast enough.

All she could do was cower in fear as the hungry crow closed in.

Friendly-Faced and Fluffy-Tailed

Just before the crow's talons could scratch Tally's shell, a ball of gray fur catapulted into view. The crow swerved and the other animal threw itself over Tally, making a vicious chittering noise. "Go!" it shouted. "Get out of here!"

The crow squawked with frustration and flew off in search of easier prey.

The animal on top of Tally let out a whoop of triumph. Then it knocked on Tally's shell. "You okay in there?"

"Mmph mmph-mmph," Tally said, unable to get a proper word out with a furry stomach covering her face.

"Sorry, what did you say?" There was a pause. "Oh." The animal moved away fast.

Tally blinked. She still felt dizzy with fear, but when she scanned the sky, there wasn't a crow in sight. There was only–

Ack! An enormous squirrel! Tally jumped sideways before she remembered the truth: the squirrel was normal-sized. Tally the turtle was just very small. Giggling both at herself and at the idea of an actual giant squirrel, Tally studied her friendly-faced and fluffy-tailed rescuer.

The squirrel stepped toward her, extending his paws. "Hello! Are you okay? That was terrifying! But amazing! Did you see the look on that thing's face when it flew off? No, of course you didn't. I was sitting on you. Well, let me tell you, it was great. I sure showed that bird who's boss. Anyway, what's your name? My name is–" The squirrel let out a bunch of chattering syllables, none of which Tally understood. "You can call me Chaz. I'm a squirrel, by the way. And you're a turtle. I love turtles!"

"My name's Tally," Tally said. "And I'm not *really* a turtle–"

"How'd you get so far from the creek? Must've taken you all morning to crawl here.

Had to bask on this particular rock, did you? I guess it is a pretty nice rock. Spectacular view." Chaz stopped talking long enough to turn in an admiring circle.

"I'm not from the creek–"

"Well, good thing for you I was here!" Chaz beamed. "Tally, you said? That's a nice name. Is it short for anything, like Chaz is?"

"Um." Tally braced herself. "It's short for Tallulah."

To Tally's surprise, Chaz didn't laugh. "Oh, I like that! I do!"

"Thanks! Me too." Tally looked over at the school. There was a different group of kids playing outside now, though it still wasn't her class. How long had she been basking, anyway? She turned back to Chaz. "Can you help me get to the sch–"

Tally groaned as a wave of hunger washed over her. She suddenly felt like she could eat an entire sausage and pepperoni pizza . . . or whatever the turtle version of pizza was. A huge pile of leaves? A bunch of—*gulp*—bugs and worms?

She thought about asking Chaz if he knew what turtles ate, but then decided she didn't care if it *was* bugs and worms. Her stomach was empty, and her mouth was so dry her tongue felt like a fuzzy caterpillar. "Food," she croaked. "Water."

Chaz jumped into action. "Okay! Yes! I will take you back to the creek!"

"That's not what I–"

"Bite my coat, and don't let go!" Chaz waited for Tally to clamp her jaw shut around a mouthful of musky gray fur. Then he took off running, with Tally clinging to his back.

12

With a Heroic Grunt

Tally bounced up and down, the bottom of her shell slapping rhythmically against Chaz's back. She was too focused on clenching her jaw to tuck her limbs away, so her feet flailed in the air. Even though she was biting down as hard as she could, she could feel Chaz's fur slip-slip-slipping through her beak.

She wasn't going to be able to hold on much longer.

Chaz suddenly skidded to a stop. Tally went flying. She tumbled over Chaz's head, did a flip, and landed in a mud puddle, belly-up.

“Oh, wow! Are you all right?” Chaz asked. “I should have warned you we were here. Well, welcome home!” When Tally didn’t say anything, Chaz turned in a fretful circle, wringing his paws. “Tell me you’re okay, Tally. Talk to me! Talk to me!”

Tally had the wind knocked out of her, but as soon as her breath came back, she gasped, “Hard to . . . get a . . . word in.”

Chaz snickered. “You’re right, I am a chatterbox. Luckily for you, I’m quite interesting to listen to. Now, you’re upside-down. What are we going to do about that? Do you want me to flip you? Do you want me to get your family, and they can flip you?"

"Let me think for a second," Tally said, trying not to sound as irritated as she felt. She hated being stuck on her back, helpless and ridiculous. And twice in one day! It was humiliating.

But Clementine hadn't laughed at her, and Chaz wasn't laughing now.

You can figure this out, Tally told herself. She wiggled her legs. She rocked from side to side and from front to back on her curved shell, testing her range of motion.

"Sure you don't want my help?" Chaz asked, venturing closer.

"Nope!" Tally said. "I want to do this on . . ." She began to rock right and left again. "My . . ." she continued, really putting her weight into the movement. "Own!"

After a few vigorous swings, she felt her two left feet tap the earth. She dropped onto her back again immediately, but she didn't give up. On the next tilt, she threw her head left. She stretched and stretched her neck, imagining that she was trying to bite a Starburst that was just out of reach. She stretched her tail left too, and she scratched her claws at the damp ground.

She teetered. She tottered. For a second, she was perfectly balanced on her left side. Then, with a heroic grunt, she tossed her right legs forward.

She landed on her feet. "I did it!"

Chaz applauded. "Good job! Did you know you could do that?"

Tally shook her head. "I told you, I'm not really a—"

Her stomach growled. She rushed into the creek. She paddled around, slurping water. She chomped on delicious plants. She even tried a few small insects. They weren't nearly as icky as she'd expected. The flavor was slightly nutty.

She ate and drank and ate and drank, and then she burped with satisfaction.

"Better?" Chaz sat on his haunches, gnawing on an acorn.

"Better." Tally swam back toward solid ground, feeling full and sleepy. She wanted to find a nice patch of sun to bask in for the rest of the afternoon. But she made herself focus. She was a person, not a turtle, and it was time to make things right.

“I need to get to the school,” Tally said. “Can you take me?”

“Why?” Chaz asked. “Aren’t you happy here?”

“It is nice,” Tally acknowledged, “but it’s not home.” She crawled over to Chaz and nudged him. “So, will you give me a ride?”

“Of course.” The squirrel crouched. “Hop on.”

What If, What If, What If?

Tally scanned the outside of the school building, looking for the windows that belonged to Mrs. Norrell's room. She remembered cheerful sunflower-print curtains. As she and Chaz barreled closer, she spotted them. The sunflowers were rustling in the breeze.

Wait. Was the window open? That could be her way in!

"Mmmph-mm-mmmph!" Tally grunted, her jaw clenched around Chaz's fur.

"What was that?" Chaz slowed to a stop, and Tally lowered herself to the ground. "Tell me what you need and I'll make it happen," Chaz said. "I'm here to help. I love helping! Talk to me, my turtle friend!"

"I keep trying to tell you, I'm not a turtle." Tally pointed a claw toward the windows. "Can you get me up to that ledge?"

"Yep!" Chaz let Tally clamber onto his back for a third time. "But what do you mean, you're not a turtle?" He began to climb a drain pipe up the side of the brick wall, which made Tally

feel like she was dangling from a steep cliff by her mouth. "You have a turtle face and a turtle shell," Chaz said. "You're greenish-brown and scaly. You have a tail."

When they reached the ledge and Tally had her feet under her again, she said, "I know I look like a turtle now, but I wasn't a turtle when I woke up this morning."

Chaz cocked his head. "What were you?"

"I was a person. A seven-year-old girl, to be exact."

Chaz was properly quiet for the first time since Tally met him. "Whoa," he finally said. "How did you end up like this?"

"I'm not sure. I was in there." Tally nodded toward the classroom. "They were all making fun of me–"

"Making fun of you?" Chaz looked horrified. "Why?"

"My name, Tallulah. They were all laughing about it. And–"

"I can't believe every single kid in your

class was laughing at you." Chaz shook his head, and then chittered angrily at the window.

"Well . . . some kids were, and some weren't," Tally admitted. "But I wasn't sure who was who. Who was nice, and who wasn't. I'm new here. My family just moved–"

"Which creek did you live at before?"

"You're not listening!" Tally was growing impatient with the constant interruptions. "I've never lived at any creek. We had a house in another town, and now we have a house in this town. I have a mom and a dad and an older sister. They're all humans, like me." She paused. "I mean, like I'm supposed to be."

Tally studied her classmates at their desks. Her eyes darted from Madison to Victoria to Nate, and then she looked down at David, who sat in the front row next to the windows. He wadded up a sheet of paper, and the second Mrs. Norrell turned her back, he threw it in an arc to Owen in the last row.

Everyone—even grouchy Victoria—looked like they *belonged*.

Was Tally going to belong here, too?

She'd felt brave and confident at the creek, with her belly full and her scaly skin cool in the water. Now, her stomach was queasy and her knees were wobbly. *Imagine something happy*, Tally told herself, but nothing came to mind. She was too busy splashing around in her troubles.

"There's someone in that room who may be able to help me change back into a person," she murmured. "I want to be me again! But . . . what if this new place is *never* as good as where I used to live? What if I *never* make new friends as wonderful as the ones I had before? What if I'm going to feel left out *forever and ever*?"

What if, what if, what if?

With a wail, Tally pulled herself inside her shell.

A Story about Acorns

After a moment alone in the darkness, Tally felt a tap, tap, tap on her back.

Chaz leaned down to peer at her through the shell's opening. "Hey," he said. Tally poked her nose out, and Chaz patted her face with a soft paw. "Can I tell you a story? It's a story about acorns! It's really good. Wanna hear it?"

"Sure," Tally mumbled.

"You know that squirrels gather acorns for the winter, right?"

"Yes."

"Before my first winter," Chaz said, "I was scared I wouldn't be able to collect enough to make it through. Also, I wanted to gather the right acorns—the best acorns. I worried and counted and worried and counted." The squirrel began to pace back and forth on the windowsill, like the memory was making him agitated. "The weather got colder and colder, and I was lying awake at night thinking about all of the acorns I hadn't gathered yet."

Tally poked her head further out of her shell. “Did everything turn out okay?”

Chaz stopped pacing. “It did. When the first snow came, I had a lot of good acorns. When I needed a few more, I had friends who were happy to help me bring them home.”

“That’s great,” Tally said, looking into her classroom again. “But . . . what does this have to do with me?”

“Worrying doesn’t help you gather acorns any faster.”

Tally frowned, confused. “I don’t need to gather acorns.”

Chaz gave her a kind smile. “It’s exhausting, expecting the worst to happen. Wouldn’t you rather expect good things?”

“Good things like what?”

“Like having enough acorns.”

“Enough acorns,” Tally repeated slowly.

“Now, expecting good things out of life doesn’t mean you don’t have to put in any work,” Chaz cautioned. “I don’t mean you’re sitting around, waiting for the acorns to land in your lap. What I mean is, you do what you can, and you try to trust that everything will turn out okay." Chaz looked at Tally expectantly, like he was waiting for applause.

But Tally still wasn't sure she understood the squirrel's point.

"When you look in that room," Chaz said, rapping a paw against the window, "what do you see? No friends? Or new friends?"

Tally opened her mouth to answer, but Chaz didn't let her speak.

"I try to see everyone I meet as a new friend. And guess what? Most of the time, I'm right!" Chaz rubbed his paws together. "On that note, let's get you turned back into a human, so you can make some new friends–besides me, I mean. We're friends, aren't we?"

"We are." About that, Tally was one hundred percent sure. "Thank you so much, Chaz. For everything."

"Thanks for being my friend!" Chaz

measured Tally's height with his tail and held the measurement up to the opening in the window. Then he wiggled under the frame with his shoulder and pushed up to give Tally an extra inch of clearance. "Get in there," he said fondly, "and don't forget to visit."

Something about This Class

Tally ducked under the raised window and found herself on one of the shelves that ran along the wall of her classroom. Her classmates were still at their desks. They were now using magnifying glasses to look at different kinds of leaves.

Tally's first thought was that she wanted to use a magnifying glass, too.

Her second thought was that the leaves looked like a tasty snack.

But she wasn't here to eat leaves. She was

here to transform back into Tally Tuttle, the human being.

"Tally!" Clementine rushed toward her and wrapped all eight legs around her in a hug. "I'm so happy to see you! How did you get up here?"

"Clementine!" Tally was overjoyed to see her spider friend. "I came in the window. What are you doing up here?"

The spider pointed with both front legs. "This is who I wanted you to meet!"

Tally looked over to see Bagel the guinea pig peering at her through the bars of his cage. "Hello, Tally," Bagel said. His voice was

squeaky, yet wise, like an old man who'd just sucked the helium out of a balloon. "I bet you've had quite an adventure."

"I have," Tally said. "How did you know?"

Bagel silently flipped the latch to his cage door. He slipped out, shutting the door behind him, and nudged Tally and Clementine behind a stack of books. "I've been in Mrs. Norrell's room for five years," he said. "I've seen dozens of kids transform."

"Dozens!" Tally exclaimed. One dozen meant twelve, so dozens, plural, was lots and lots of kids. "You mean I'm not the only one?"

"Far from it," the guinea pig said.

"Do they always turn into turtles?" Clementine asked, sounding fascinated.

"No, each child is different," Bagel said.

"How did I transform?" Tally asked. "And why?"

"How?" Bagel shrugged. "I have no idea. There's just something about Mrs. Norrell's class. As for why . . ." He leaned in and gave Tally a keen look. "You tell me. Every kid has had a reason—whether they knew it or not. What happened to you today? Did you learn anything? Did anything surprise you? Did you surprise yourself?"

Tally thought about how nervous she'd been to meet her new classmates this morning. She thought about how awful it had felt to be teased, and how she'd wished she could magically disguise herself to escape.

Then she thought about being brave with Clementine when they were both scared to come out from under the bookshelf. She thought about flipping herself from her back to her front, by the creek. She thought about Chaz's story—about choosing to expect good things. And she thought about how quickly she'd become friends with both the spider and the squirrel, despite meeting them under very, very unusual circumstances.

She let all of those thoughts float around inside her until she came to one crystal-clear realization:

"It was nice having a shell to hide in. But . . . I don't think I need it anymore."

"Well, then," Bagel said with a satisfied nod.

"Can you tell me how to change back?" Tally asked.

"Not exactly," Bagel answered.

"Oh, no." Tally slumped. Had she come this far for nothing?

"Chin up. Not one kid has ended up stuck as an animal. You won't, either." Bagel gave Tally's shell an encouraging pat. "Here's what I know: In order for the magic to do its thing, you have to return to the spot where you first transformed. Not somewhere close by." The guinea pig held up a curved claw in warning. "The exact location. In five years, I've never seen it work any other way."

Tally glanced at the square of tile floor between her desk and Nate's, next to her mint-green backpack. "Okay. Then what?"

"Then . . ." Bagel said slowly, "it's up to you."

"It's up to me." Tally liked the sound of that. She smiled at Bagel. "Thank you."

Bagel beamed. "What are class pets for?"

16

A Happy Turtle Grin

Bagel led Tally to a notch cut into the back of the shelf behind his cage. "Three years ago," he said, "Lulu Lawrence turned into a lizard. I was trying to help her, but I was up here, and she was on the floor. Long story short, afterward, she made me this."

Tally crawled to the edge. "A slide! Mrs. Norrell doesn't know?"

"Not yet–so try not to scream too loud as you go down," Bagel said with a chuckle.

Tally stretched out her neck. She could only see a couple inches of the cardboard slide before it vanished into darkness. She liked slides, but she also liked seeing where she was going.

You can do this, she thought, preparing to kick off.

Bagel stopped her with a paw on her shoulder. "You can't talk to your classmates about what happened to you today. At least, not until they've had an animal day of their own."

"Why not?" Tally asked.

"Unfortunately, if a child knows it's coming, it won't happen to them." Bagel sighed. "We learned that the hard way."

"Oh." Tally gulped. "Will I know if someone has transformed?"

"You won't see it happen. Humans never do. But you'll figure it out." Bagel gave her a stern look. "Now, promise to keep the secret."

"I promise." Tally looked back at Clementine. "I'll miss you," she told the spider. "You're my first friend here."

"I'll miss you, too." Clementine hugged Tally's neck. "But you're about to make so many more friends!"

"You're right," Tally said with a shiver of anticipation. "I am."

She pushed off with her back feet. The slide was straight. The slope was steep. Tally's shell was slick. She slid *fast*.

It was fun!

She hit the floor and began to crawl. She'd made it halfway across the room when—

"Whoa! Look at that!" Nate was pointing at her. "It's a turtle!

"Ew," Victoria said, wrinkling her nose.

"It's so cute!" squealed a girl Tally didn't know yet.

Everyone crowded around.

Tally kept crawling, trying to tune out the

chatter. She knew she could get scooped up and taken outside again, or put in a cage . . . or worse. Bagel had said no kid ever stayed an animal permanently, but Tally didn't want to be the first.

"Let me through, kids," Mrs. Norrell said, making a path with her hands. She knelt in front of Tally. "Well! What are we going to do with you?"

Tally trembled, but she didn't stop moving forward.

"Maybe this is one of the other teachers' class pets," Mrs. Norrell said. "Oh, dear. Maybe I shouldn't have taken that other turtle outside, after all." She leaned in. "Don't be afraid, little one. I'll get you somewhere safe. Madison, can you hand me a tissue, please?"

"Why do you need a tissue?" someone asked. "Are you allergic?"

Mrs. Norrell laughed. "No, it's not that. Sometimes, turtles carry salmonella."

“That’s a germ that makes you sick to your stomach,” David informed the group.

“The tissue is to cover my fingers,” Mrs. Norrell explained, as Madison ran over to the arts and crafts corner.

Tally finally reached the correct floor tile. Immediately, she wished to be herself again. She pictured her jean shorts and green T-shirt and green-and-white sneakers. She pictured her straight brown hair in its ponytail and her round glasses perched on her nose. She pictured the clear sparkle polish on her fingernails.

Nothing happened.

High above Tally’s head, Madison passed Mrs. Norrell a whole box of Kleenex. Tally’s time was almost up.

She looked at Madison, and then around at all of her classmates. She imagined introducing herself properly. She imagined sitting at a crowded lunch table, telling jokes and sharing secrets. She imagined having her new friends over to her new house for a sleepover.

Her lips turned up in a happy turtle grin.

The transformation began.

17

Ready to Be Seen

The odor of rotten eggs wafted through the air, chased by the fresh scent of citrus fruit. Invisible piano keys played a tinkly tune, which was cut off by the loud *pop* of a sticky jar lid. A gust of wind pushed Tally sideways and spun her around. Then everything was still and quiet.

Tally blinked. Immediately, she knew she was person-sized. But what did she look like? She held up her hands and wiggled her fingers. Her skin was no longer scaly and striped in green, yellow, and brown. She had sparkly nails, not grimy claws. She tapped at her face. Her eyes, nose, and mouth were all in their usual spots. She twisted her arms to run her fingers over her back. She no longer had a thick, protective shell.

She was herself again!

Her classmates were emerging from their

magical fog. They seemed a little confused, just like when she'd first transformed. For a long moment, nobody spoke.

Then David squinted at Tally. She tensed, wondering if he'd remember the turtle they'd all been staring at a minute ago. Instead, he slowly said, "Ta-*loooo*-lah?"

"Ta-*loooo*-lah!" Owen crowed back.

"Actually," Tally said, her voice only a little shaky, "I go by Tally."

Mrs. Norrell was staring at the floor with a wrinkle between her eyebrows. She looked like she knew there was something she'd forgotten, but she couldn't think of what it might be. "Tallu–I mean, Tally," she said. "You've returned from the nurse's office."

Tally felt a little thrill at her teacher's words. She'd missed almost a whole school day, and no one knew! Well, she was back now, and she was on a mission.

"Are you feeling better?" Mrs. Norrell asked.

“Yes,” Tally said honestly. There were still a few butterflies in her stomach, but she wasn't going to let them win. This morning, Tally had wanted to hide. Now, she was ready to be seen. “Mrs. Norrell, can I . . .” She drew herself up as tall as she could. “Can I introduce myself to the class, since I'm new here?”

“Of course,” her teacher said. “Take your seats, kids!”

The class got settled. The room fell silent. Everyone stared at Tally, waiting for her to speak.

Tally's mouth felt dry. Her fingers felt trembly. She licked her lips and clasped her hands together. She took in a deep breath and held it, counting down in her mind: *three, two, one . . . blast-off!*

“Hi. I'm Tally Tuttle. My family moved here last week, because my mom got a new job. I think she works with Madison's dad now—hi, Madison!” A few rows up, Madison gave a friendly wave. “My favorite color is green,”

Parts of a leaf
vein
tip

Tally went on, "my favorite vegetable is corn on the cob, and my favorite candy is Starbursts. I like riding my scooter and reading books about kids going on epic adventures. I'm named after a film star who died a long time ago. My parents really like old movies."

Most of her classmates were smiling—although Victoria wore a scowl. But Tally tried to ignore the other girl's sour face. She didn't need to be best friends with every single person in the class. A few new friends would do.

She didn't need every single acorn. She just needed enough.

No Turtle Shell Required

When she finally sat down, Tally felt like she'd run a marathon. She was exhausted, but also jingly-jangly with excitement. She wasn't sure if she would rather have a dance party or take a long nap.

Instead of doing either of those things, she snuck her hand into her backpack to get a celebratory Starburst. No, after the day she'd had, she deserved *two* Starbursts. She held the candies tight in her fist. *Red and orange*, she predicted, and when she opened her fingers under her desk, she was pleased to see she was right. She unwrapped the Starbursts and ate them together, letting the flavors swirl in her mouth just like the happiness and relief that swirled inside her.

Nate tapped her on the arm. At first, she was worried he'd seen her sneaking candy. Would he tell on her? Did he want a Starburst for himself? Tally was about to say she was glad to share when he handed her a note.

"For me?" Tally whispered.

"Any other Tally Tuttles in here?" he asked, but not in a mean way.

"Ha. Thanks." Tally unfolded the sheet of paper. It was from Madison! The note read:

Hi, Tally! It's so nice to meet you! Love, Madison.

P.S. My favorite color is sky blue, and Lydia's is fire-engine red.

Tally looked up to see Madison grinning at her. Tally beamed back.

Then she looked over at Bagel's cage by the

windows. The guinea pig was looking right at her. Tally gave him a grateful thumbs-up. He nodded, turned in a tight circle, and curled up in his wood shavings for a snooze.

The next hour passed quickly. Mrs. Norrell had everyone work on creating self-portraits for their bulletin board, using whatever art supplies they wanted. They were allowed to push their desks together, so Tally formed a triangle with Madison and Lydia. While she made a collage of her face out of tissue paper

and glue, they told her a little bit about each of her classmates.

Aaron had a sweet tooth, so if Tally needed an emergency Starburst, he was the kid to ask. Zeke was short for Ezekiel, just like Tally was short for Tallulah. Nate never went anywhere without a book. Riley was a gymnast. David was constantly getting into trouble, and Owen went along with whatever David wanted to do. Gavin was the class clown. Victoria didn't seem to find *anything* funny.

By the end of the day, Tally knew so many new things. The most important new thing she'd learned was that she was going to fit in here. Her life was different than before, but different didn't have to mean bad. New wasn't always scary. Sitting between Madison and Lydia, in a room full of people she now saw as possible new friends, Tally felt comfortable, cozy, and safe.

No turtle shell required.

Ten Fun Facts about Painted Turtles

What's the difference between a turtle and a tortoise? Both are reptiles, but tortoises live on land while turtles spend at least part of their time in the water. Also, turtles tend to have smooth, flat shells and webbed feet with long claws, while tortoises often have dome-shaped shells and short, sturdy feet and legs.

Tally Tuttle turns into a painted turtle, one of the most common turtle species in North America. You can identify a painted turtle by the red, yellow, and orange markings on its black or greenish-brown skin. The top part of the shell is usually dark green, brown, or black. Some types of painted turtle have bright red, yellow, and orange markings on their undersides, while others have a bottom shell that is plain brown or tan.

A turtle's shell is part of its skeleton! The top of the shell, called the carapace, is fused to the turtle's spine and ribs. The bottom of the shell, the plastron, is connected to the carapace by bony structures called bridges, which run between the front and hind legs on either side.

The outermost layer of a turtle's shell is made up of scales called scutes, which are made of keratin–the same protein that's in your hair and fingernails! A turtle will naturally shed its scutes to make way for larger ones as it grows.

A full-grown painted turtle is six to eight inches long. As a juvenile turtle, Tally is only four or five inches long. It's no wonder she's worried about being stepped on!

6

When she goes outside, Tally feels a strong urge to bask in the sunlight. Soaking up the sun helps turtles regulate their body temperature. Basking can also help turtles shed scutes and get rid of parasites, like leeches.

Mrs. Norrell is right when she tells David and Owen that turtles' shells protect them from many predators, but certain animals still pose a danger. Tally is attacked by a crow, but turtles must also keep an eye out for alligators, hawks, bald eagles, foxes, and raccoons.

8

When Tally uses her legs and her long, flexible neck to flip herself right side up at the creek, she's doing exactly what a real turtle would do. Turtles who land on their backs are vulnerable, so they instinctively work to right themselves.

9

Painted turtles are omnivores. That means they eat both plants, like leaves and algae, and animals, such as small insects, fish, and crustaceans. They feed by hunting along water bottoms and by skimming the surface of the water. Instead of teeth, painted turtles have tough, horny plates in their jaws for gripping and mashing food.

10

Tally may only be a turtle for a few hours, but real turtles can live a very long time. Painted turtles that are properly cared for in captivity can live twenty to thirty years. Some painted turtles make it to their forties or fifties!

Acknowledgments

Thanks to:

- My agent, Alyssa Eisner Henkin, for encouraging me to try writing chapter books and for helping me find the right story to tell.
- My editor, Erica Finkel, for making the manuscript shine.
- Ariel Landy, Johanna Tarkela, Marcie Lawrence, and Deena Fleming, for their beautiful illustrations and design work.
- The rest of the team at Amulet Books: Megan Carlson, Jenn Jimenez, Emily Daluga, Maggie Lehrman, and Andrew Smith, for taking great care of me and Tally.
- Janae Marks and Lance Rubin, for their early feedback (and their friendship!).
- Herpetologist John Iverson, for sharing painted turtle factoids.

- Ian McKay, for giving his professional insight into childhood anxiety.
- My family and friends, for their support along this publishing journey.
- Justin and Evie—the two of you are my most magical adventure.

About the Author

Kathryn Holmes always dreamed of telling stories for a living. These days, she writes books for kids and teens. Originally from Maryville, Tennessee, she went to Goucher College in Baltimore, Maryland, where she majored in dance and English literature. She later received her MFA in Writing for Children from the New School in New York City. Kathryn now lives in Brooklyn, New York, with her husband and daughter. You can find her online at www.kathrynholmes.com.

About the Author

Kathryn Holmes always dreamed [illegible] [illegible] a [illegible] Table days she [illegible] [illegible] originally from [illegible]ville, Tennessee [illegible] went to [illegible] College [illegible] [illegible] [illegible] [illegible] English [illegible] [illegible] received [illegible] [illegible] [illegible] [illegible] [illegible] [illegible] [illegible] [illegible] [illegible] lives in [illegible] [illegible] [illegible] [illegible] [illegible] [illegible] [illegible] [illegible] www.[illegible].com